Almu… …dt

…EN

GTON

…U

ARRIVED AND WE BECAME A FAMILY...

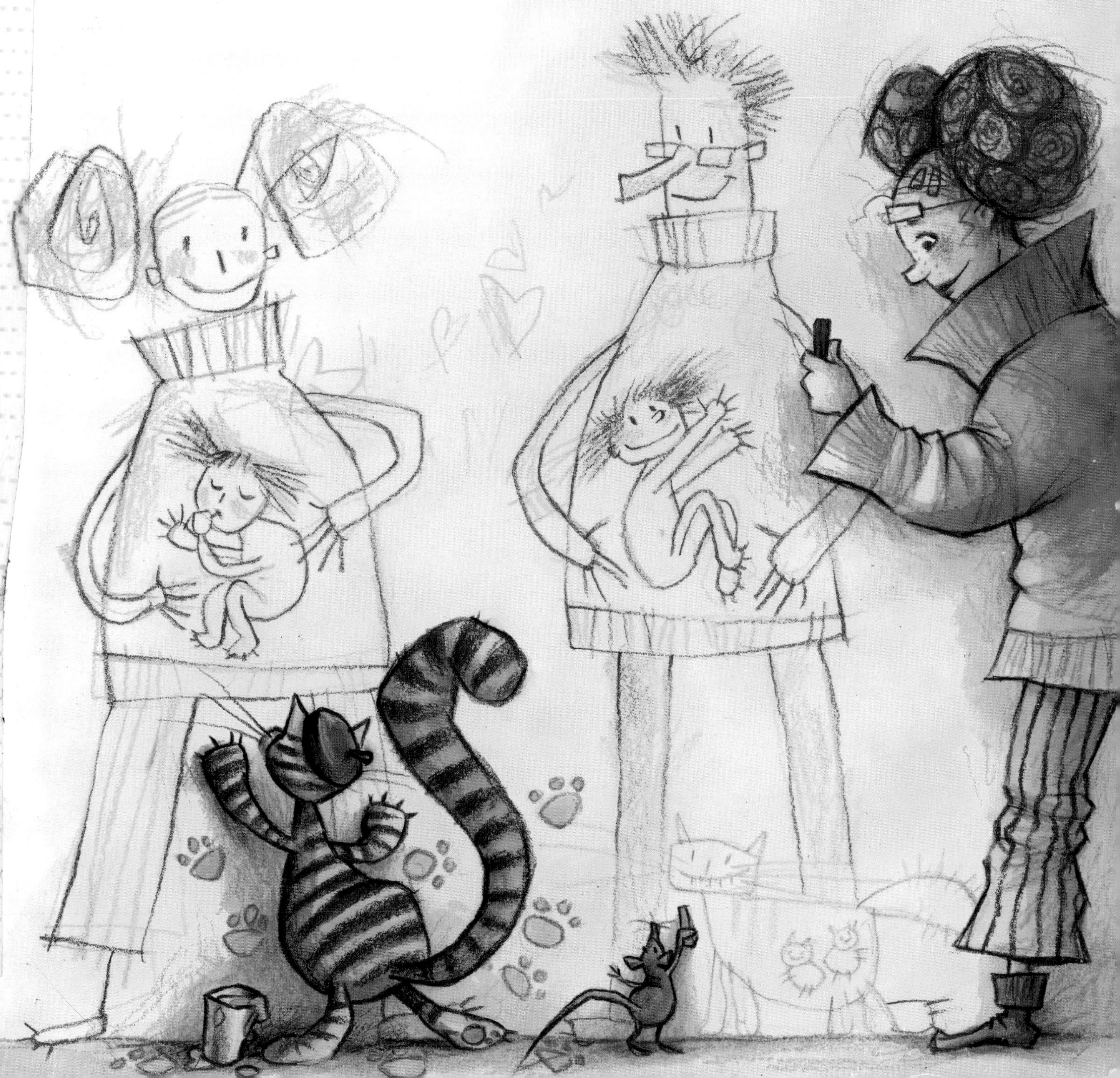

FOR CAROLINA, DENISA AND ANNELI

AND FOR ADOPTED BOYS

KUCKUCK

PIP

PIP

FOR HELGA, RENATE AND KALLIE WHO WERE ALSO ADOPTED

FOR CONRAD AND THE RABBIT LISA'S ADOPTED ANIMALS !!!

AND THEN YOU ARRIVED AND WE BECAME A FAMILY...

Written by Anette Hildebrandt

Illustrated by Almud Kunert

Translated by Reinhard Lindner

Perwas Press

This is Lisa. Lisa can already ride a scooter. She can draw figures with hair, ears and fingers on their hands. But her favourite thing is painting her family, Mum, Dad, the cat Conrad and, of course, Lisa herself. However, today she is bored. "Lisa, what's the matter?" asks Mum from her office. "Don't you want to play?" Lisa shakes her head. Perhaps she would like to play picture lotto with Mum, if Mum had enough time. But Mum has to work on the computer. Or maybe she would like to play princesses with Mum, read a book or just sit on Mum's lap. Or would she like to do something else? Lisa thinks.

When her Mum finishes her work, Dad comes home. Lisa loves it when Dad comes home from work. He spreads his arms out and Lisa runs towards him and, if Mum and Conrad are also there, then they are a family, with Lisa right in the middle. Suddenly Lisa knows exactly what she wants: "Please, tell me again how I came to you!" she asks Mum and Dad. Then she goes and gets her life story book with a heart on the cover.

Lisa snuggles up between her parents. She is happy. The story of how she came to Mum and Dad a long time ago is a very special story. It is her story, and it is the story of her family. Lisa waits excitedly. Then her Mum opens the book and starts to talk:

"Many, many years ago, when you were not even born, we wanted to have a baby. We wanted to be a family. But even though we wanted this very badly, nothing happened in my tummy. Absolutely nothing. It made us sad. After some time we had another thought: perhaps there was a child somewhere who didn't have a Mum and Dad to care for them. That gave us a fantastic idea.

First thing the next day we went to Social Services, where people help adults and children with their problems. We said: 'We would like to be a Mum and Dad to a child who needs new parents.' The lady, who listened to us, was very friendly. She called our plan Adopting a Child and thought she would be able to help us. She would look for a child who needed us – a child who we could care for. But we had to wait for a very long time! We had to be very patient! Because of this, we dreamt of you and waited and waited.

And the child we wanted was you.

Finally, one day – I remember it very clearly! I was cooking pasta – the lady from Social Services rang. She said: 'I have a child for you. She is called Lisa.' Whaaat? Suddenly thousands of butterflies danced in my tummy. And I began to dance, too, – and didn't see that the pasta was boiling over.

And the child, who made me dizzy with happiness, was you.

Dad and I could not wait to see you, but before then we had to do a lot of things! We bought bottles, toys and a dummy for you – three trolleys full of things. The lady at the shop was astonished.

Then we furnished your room. You got Dad's old wardrobe that he had had when he was a child and Granny brought you my old pink cot in which I slept when I was a baby.

And the child, who would soon live with us, was you.

Finally, the day arrived when we could pick you up. Dad squeezed my hand and I squeezed his hand and like that we went to see you. We looked nervously into your cot, and the little girl that we saw, who looked up at us and showed us her rattle, was you, with little hands and an even smaller nose.

The sweetest baby we had ever seen!

I took you very carefully into my arms. I asked you:
'Can I be your new Mum and care for you?' And how
did you answer? You were not yet able to speak! You
just – smiled.
Then I cuddled you, kissed your little hands, then your
little feet, and Dad constantly stroked your face.
The baby, who gently snuggled up to us, was you.
I became your Mum, and Dad became your Dad.

On the way home I sat on the backseat with you. This meant that
I was very close to you. We played 'poke-mum-in-the-nose'. You
gurgled and squeaked happily and my nose became very red.

After a while, you were hungry and I gave my new baby a bottle for the very first time. Dad was amazed how noisily you drank and I was astonished how content you were. And the child, who came home with us, was you.

When we arrived home, Dad carried you very carefully over the doorstep. Conrad immediately came and sniffed curiously at your feet. 'This is Lisa, our baby,' we explained to Conrad. 'She now belongs to us, for ever.'

And the child, who fell asleep in Dad's arms, was you.

"THIS IS
A CURL FROM
YOUR FIRST
HAIRCUT."

"ON THIS PHOTO
YOU ARE A BIT
EXCITED
IT IS YOUR FIRST DAY
AT THE NURSERY."

ING,
DAY."

Lisa's Mum smiles.
"And the child, we are
so proud of, is you," she
says. "But now I am
already sooo big!" Lisa
jumps up and throws her arms
up in the air. "Yes, we have a big
child now," answers Dad with a
smile and closes the life story book.

Lisa climbs back on the sofa to her place between Mum and Dad.
Yes, here she feels happy and secure to think about everything.
She has known for a long time that she was not in Mum's tummy,
that's absolutely clear! But, she thinks, perhaps it would have been
nice to have been in her tummy, and she says quietly to
Mum: "I think, I would have liked to be in your
tummy for a little bit." – "Yes," replies Mum, "I
would have liked it too! Then I would have
tapped my tummy and said: Hello, my
baby, how are you inside my
tummy?"

"That would have been funny!" Lisa has to laugh. And then she remembers that she was in somebody else's tummy. In the tummy of her first Mum, who had given birth to her, but Lisa doesn't remember this at all. Not even, when she tries very hard.

But perhaps Mum knows what happened, and Lisa asks: "The lady, who gave birth to me: Why didn't she want me?" – "She wanted to keep you!" answers Mum. "She loved you very much. But she was very poor and didn't have a job. So she didn't have enough money for herself and a little baby. So she had to work very hard and learn a lot, too, and nobody was there to help her." Lisa nods thoughtfully and Dad explains further:

"She felt very unhappy and was very worried about you. So she wanted you to be with a family with a Mum and Dad who could take care of you." Lisa snuggles up to her parents for a while. She thinks very hard about her first Mum. "I think…," she says at last, "she did the right thing."

Suddenly she jumps off the sofa and disappears into her room. Lisa has an idea! She wants to draw a picture of her first Mum with the new crayons she got from Granny. When she finishes it, she carefully cuts the picture out and shows it to her parents. Mum and Dad are overwhelmed.

"Would you like to put it into your life story book?" asks Dad. Lisa nods, and together with Mum she sticks the lady, who gave birth to her, into the big book with the heart. Lisa is very happy.

"Now they are all in it," she says.

Zerwas Press
4 Stourwood Mansions
Stourwood Avenue
Bournemouth
BH6 3PP

First published in the UK in 2005

Title of the original German edition:
Und dann kamst du und wir wurden eine Familie
© 2003 Ravensburger Buchverlag Otto Maier GmbH
Ravensburg (Germany)

English text © 2005 Reinhard Lindner

ISBN 0 9531830 3 3

A CIP catalogue record for this book is available from The British Library

Printed & bound by Pims Print, UK